Aunt Connie's Favorite Animals on the Farm

PAGE PUBLISHING, INC.
New York, NY

First originally published by Page Publishing, Inc. 2019

ISBN 978-1-64350-624-1 (Paperback)
ISBN 978-1-64350-625-8 (Digital)

Printed in the United States of America

Aunt Connie's Favorite Animals on the Farm

Connie Collins

You're beautiful, Poncho Pony!!

I wish you had a saddle
So I could take a ride.
We would trot along the trail
And see the countryside!

"Moooo," says Mrs. Queenie Cow!

I don't know how you give the milk
That my mom buys at the store.
Your calf is such a frisky pet…
That makes me love you more!

Waddle, waddle, Dilly Duck!

Your little ducklings follow you
When you say, "Quack! Quack!"
They might try to run away
But they always come right back!

Arf! Arf! Shaggy Puppy!

You love to run and chase the ball…
We have fun when we play.
I'm lucky that you live with me
So we can play all day!

Meow! Miss Kellyn Kitty Cat!

How I adore your little kittens!
Shh…just listen to them purr.
They're all so soft and cuddly…
May I gently stroke their fur?

Hi there, teeny Tatum Turtle!

It's cool that you live in a shell
But can you come out to play?
I'll be very, very quiet
So I won't scare you away!

"Baa, baa, baa," says woolly Sarah Sheep!

Do you know the little song
About Mary and her lamb?
If you will help me sing it,
I'll say, "Thank you, ma'am!"

Good morning, Rodney Rooster!

You wake up early every day
With your "Cock-a-doodle-do!"
When I know that you're awake,
I want to wake up, too!

Here's funny Fiddle Faddle Frog!

I like to listen to your "ribbit,"
And you're awesome when you leap.
When I saw you on the lily pad,
I thought you were asleep!

"Oink, oink!" says Petunia Pig!

Along with your eight babies,
Do you live on this farm?
You'd better stay inside your pen
So your piglets won't be harmed.

What's up, Tyler Turkey?

Twiddle-dee-dee, twiddle-dee-dum
And how are you today?
When you just "gobble-gobble,"
I don't know what you say!

Here comes Noah Night Crawler!

You never, ever make a sound…
All you do is wiggle.
When you're crawling on my arm,
It makes me want to giggle!

About the Author

The most significant personal aspects of my life are being a follower of Christ, wife, mother, and grandmother.

Divine inspiration enables me to appreciate the beauty of nature and to enjoy the magnificence of God's creation. The opportunities to travel both at home and abroad have opened up this incredible world to me. Creative thinking and writing enable me to escape the daily grind and to record life's events from a personal point of view. Life is good because every day is a blessing!